A NOTE TO PARENTS

Congratulations on choosing the best in educational materials for your child. By selecting our top-quality products, you can be assured that the concepts used in our books will reinforce and enhance the skills that are being taught in classrooms nationwide.

And what better way to get young readers excited than with Mercer Mayer's Little Critter, a character loved by children everywhere? Our First Readers offer simple and engaging stories about Little Critter that children can read on their own. Each level incorporates reading skills, colorful illustrations, and challenging activities.

Level 1 – The stories are simple and use repetitive language. Illustrations are highly supportive.
Level 2 - The stories begin to grow in complexity. Language is still repetitive, but it is mixed with more challenging vocabulary.
Level 3 - The stories are more complex. Sentences are longer and more varied.

To help your child make the most of this book, look at the first few pictures in the story and discuss what is happening. Ask your child to predict where the story is going. Then, once your child has read the story, have him or her review the word list and do the activities. This will reinforce vocabulary words from the story and build reading comprehension.

You are your child's first and most influential teacher. No one knows your child the way you do. Tailor your time together to reinforce a newly acquired skill or to overcome a temporary stumbling block. Praise your child's progress and ideas, take delight in his or her imagination, and most of all, enjoy your time together!

Library of Congress Cataloging-in-Publication Data

Mayer, Mercer, 1943–
    The little Christmas tree/by Mercer Mayer.
        p.cm.--(First Readers; level 2)
    "Grades K–1."
    Summary: The Christmas tree that Dad brings home is a little skimpy, but
    each family member has as an idea for what will make it better, until
    Little Critter finally adds the crowning touch.
    ISBN 1-57768-583-0 (pbk.)
    [1. Christmas trees--Fiction. 2. Christmas decorations--Fiction. 3. Family
    life--Fiction.] I.Title.

    PZ7.M462Lae 2004
    [E]--dc22

                                                         2003056219

School Specialty
Children's Publishing

Text Copyright © 2004 School Specialty Children's Publishing. Published by Gingham Dog
Press, an imprint of School Speciality Children's Publishing, a member of the School
Specialty family.
Art Copyright © 2004 Mercer Mayer.

Send all inquiries to:
School Specialty Children's Publishing
8720 Orion Place
Columbus, OH 43240-2111

Printed in the United States of America.
1-57768-583-0

 A Big Tuna Trading Company, LLC/J. R. Sansevere Book

3 4 5 6 7 8 9 10 PHXBK 09 08 07 06 05 04

FIRST READERS

Level **2**   Grades **K–1**

THE LITTLE CHRISTMAS TREE

by Mercer Mayer

GINGHAM DOG
PRESS

Columbus, Ohio

Dad brought home a Christmas tree.
It was small and skinny.
"That tree needs help," said Little Sister.

Mom had an idea. We baked
gingerbread cookies. We put them
on the tree.
"The tree still needs help," said Mom.

7

8

Grandma had an idea. We made paper snowflakes. We put them on the tree.

"The tree still needs help," said Grandma.

Little Sister had an idea.
We made bows.

We put them on the tree.
"The tree still needs help,"
said Little Sister.

Grandpa had an idea. We made strings of popcorn and cranberries. We put them on the tree.

"The tree still needs help," said Grandpa.

Dad said, "I like the popcorn and the cranberries. I like the bows. I like the snowflakes and the cookies. But, the tree still needs help."

"I have an idea!" said Little Critter.

15

Little Critter knew just what the little tree needed. It was their best Christmas tree ever.

Word List

Read each word in the lists below. Then, find each word in the story. Now, make up a new sentence using the word. Say your sentence out loud.

Words I Know
bows
cookies
help
paper
small
tree

Challenge Words
cranberries
gingerbread
idea
popcorn
snowflakes
strings

Compound Words

Compound words are two words that make up one word.

Example:

snow   +   man   =   snowman

Point to a word in the column on the left. Then, point to the word in the column on the right that helps to make a compound word.

ginger   flakes

some   corn

snow   thing

pop   bread

ABC Order

On a separate sheet of paper, write each set of words in abc order. Look at the first letter in each word to help you.

tree

idea

cookies

- - - - - - - - - - -

snowflakes

better

missing

What Happened?

In what order did Little Critter and his family decorate the little tree? Point to each picture to show what happened first, second, third, fourth, and last.

Comprehension Quiz

Answer these questions. Try
not to look back at the story.

Who said the little tree needed help first?

What did Mom want to put on the little tree?

What did Grandma want to put on the little tree?

What color were the bows?

What did Little Critter think the tree needed?

Vocabulary Quiz

Point to each word that names the picture below it.

paper   puppy   pig

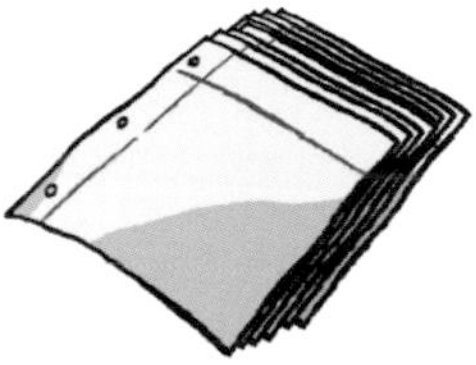

baby   bug   bow

see   stay   star

truck   tree   toy

23

Answer Key

page 19
Compound Words

gingerbread

something

snowflakes

popcorn

page 20
ABC Order

cookies
idea
tree

better
missing
snowflakes

page 21
What Happened?

Little Critter and his family decorated the little tree in this order:

1. gingerbread cookies
2. snowflakes
3. red bows
4. popcorn strings
5. star

page 22
Comprehension Quiz

1. Little Sister said the little tree needed help first.
2. Mom wanted to put gingerbread cookies on the tree.
3. Grandma wanted to put snowflakes on the tree.
4. The bows were red.
5. Little Critter thought the tree needed a star at the top.

page 23
Vocabulary Quiz

paper

bow

star

tree